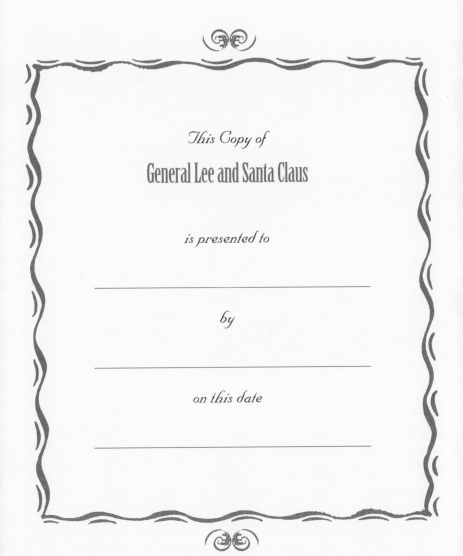

This Copy of

General Lee and Santa Claus

is presented to

_____

by

_____

on this date

_____

General Lee
~ and ~
Santa Claus

An Adaptation

General Lee
~ and ~
Santa Claus

An Adaptation

— by —

Randall Bedwell

Spiridon Press
Nashville

General Lee and Santa Claus
— *An Adaptation* —
by Randall Bedwell

Managing Editor: Carol Boker ~ Associate Editors: Trent Booker and Palmer Jones
Illustrations: Jean Holmgren ~ Layout and Design: Greg Hastings ~ Creative Director: Pat Patterson
Patterson Graham Design Group, Memphis, Tennessee

ISBN 1-889709-01-8

Library of Congress Cataloging-In-Publication Data

97-60758

*Spiridon Press wishes to acknowledge the Virginia
Historical Society and the Robert E. Lee Memorial Association
for their support in the publication of this book.*

A royalty from the sale of this book is donated to Stratford Hall, birthplace of Robert E. Lee.

General Lee and Santa Claus, as well as other titles produced by Spiridon Press
may be purchased at special discounts for fund-raising, educational, or sales promotion
use. Contact Spridon Press, Inc., Post Office Box 120969, Nashville, Tennessee 37212

For additional copies of this book, call 1-800-472-0438

First Printing

5   4   3   2   1

Spiridon Press
Post Office Box 120969
Nashville, Tennessee 37212
Visit our website at www.spiridon.com

General Lee and Santa Claus is a registered trademark of Spiridon Press, Inc.

General Lee and Santa Claus
— An Adaptation —

Introduction

The original *General Lee and Santa Claus* was printed in 1867, just two years after General Robert E. Lee surrendered his Confederate troops to General Ulysses S. Grant and the Union Army. Anticipating the unique position destined for Lee in the pantheon of our national heroes, author Louise Clack created a story attesting to the admiration and affection Southerners felt for their general, as well as accurately projecting his new role as the mitigator of Southern defeat. Moreover, by pairing Lee with Santa Claus, the most unlikely of partners, Mrs. Clack not only preserved an otherwise obscure oral tradition, but also created a delightful holiday story for children.

In 1996, General Lee and Santa Claus was reprinted by Guild Bindery Press, Inc. After a review of the book appeared in *Southern Living* magazine, the public responded enthusiastically and the reprint sold in large quantities. Many people were delighted with the book in its original form. However, there also were an overwhelming number of requests for an updated version, one that was more readily understood by today's children.

The request has been met in the following pages. Here, you will find *General Lee and Santa Claus, An Adaptation*. Rendered into language more easily understood by today's children, yet nonetheless true to the original, the story has roots that are still discernible. The narrative remains prompted by the request: "Please General Lee, tell us if Santa Claus loves the little Rebel children." The story line still features a trio of fantastic dreams reminiscent of the ghostly visitations in Charles Dicken's *A Christmas Carol*, a tale that strongly influences our celebration of the holiday season even today. *General Lee and Santa Claus* remains a timeless Christmas classic for children—but now it is also for the children of today.

Randall Bedwell
Nashville, Tennessee
March 1997

Chapter 1

Three Hopeful Sisters

It was early December in 1865. Like most young children, Lutie, Minnie, and Birdie were looking forward to Christmas. Santa Claus had not visited them in four years. Yet Lutie, Minnie, and Birdie thought that perhaps this year would be different. The Civil War had finally ended in April, and life looked brighter for the three little girls.

The girls lived in a big old house in a small town in Mississippi. Their Aunt Sarah took care of them because their mother was ill and had to stay in her bed. Lutie was 9 years old, a plump child with rosy red cheeks. She had brown hair and sparkling brown eyes. She almost always carried a book in her hands. Reading was her favorite pastime.

Birdie, who was 5 years old, also had brown hair and brown eyes like her oldest sister. Instead of reading, Birdie spent her days playing with her dolls. Sometimes she acted mischievously, just like a little elf. Belinda was her real name, not Birdie. Her mother got sick when she was only a year old. Everyone said she was like a little birdie left all alone. That's how she got her nickname.

Seven-year-old Minnie had bright blue eyes that twinkled. She loved to run, dance, and play tricks. It was hard to get mad at Minnie. After she played a trick on someone, she always gave them a little kiss and promised to be good. Minnie really did have a good heart. Sometimes she stopped playing and went to a quiet spot to say her prayers.

One day Minnie was sitting on the porch with Lutie and Birdie. She had dressed her cat in a doll's dress and was rocking it to sleep. It was a bright winter day. The birds were chirping happily. "I just realized why the birds sing better than we do," she said. "It is because they fly so near to heaven that they catch the angels' voices. I am going to ask God to lend me some wings. I want to go catch the pretty notes too. Then I can sing like the robins and the mockingbirds."

"I just realized why the birds sing better than we do," she said.

"It is because they fly so near to heaven that they catch the angels' voices."

"Oh, Minnie, please ask for some wings for me too, won't you?" begged Birdie. But Minnie didn't hear her question. She was too busy scolding her cat for not going to sleep like a good baby.

No matter what else Minnie was doing, she was always thinking about their father. He had marched off to fight for the South during the Civil War. He worked as a spotter for the Confederate army. He flew high in a hot-air balloon to look for Union troops. One day Union soldiers shot down his balloon. The army could not find him but thought that he had probably died in the fall. No one had heard from him in almost two years. He loved all the girls, but Minnie knew she was his favorite. Her blue eyes twinkled just like his. Oh, how she missed him.

Minnie said she did not care what the big people in the South did. She would never have given up to the North. Her friends did not want her to be angry at her enemies. Whenever they said anything about it, Minnie asked, "Have you forgotten my beautiful Papa?" Then she went away and said her prayers.

Like everyone else in the South, Minnie thought General Robert E. Lee was a wonderful man. One day, Aunt Sarah told her a story about him, hoping that it might teach her a lesson:

> A young girl lived near Appomattox Court House where General Lee surrendered to General Grant. When the girl saw what was happening, she ran to General Lee and hugged him. She cried, "Oh, General, General! Is this really happening?" He looked at her for a moment, while big tears ran down his cheeks. He raised his hand to heaven, and spoke in a clear, low voice: "Accept it, my child. God knows best."

When Aunt Sarah finished the story, Minnie asked, "Did General Lee really say that?"

"Yes," replied her aunt.

"Well, then, Aunt Sarah," said Minnie, "I will promise to say so, too, because General Lee is a wise man."

Chapter 2

Where Is Santa Claus?

One chilly evening, when Aunt Sarah was tucking
the girls into bed, they talked about Christmas.
Being the oldest, Lutie remembered when the
candles twinkled throughout the house and
greenery covered the mantels of the fireplaces.
She told the other girls about Mama and Papa
dancing around the big Christmas tree in
the hallway.

"It's time to get to sleep now," said Aunt Sarah.
"Dream about Santa Claus. He will arrive in a
few weeks."

Minnie said, "I don't want to give any of my
dreams to Santa because he wasn't a Rebel.

He didn't care about any of us. He didn't bring presents to the Southern children for four Christmases. He probably only cares about the children in the North."

"There was a blockade during the war," said Lutie. "People and supplies could not get through because the Union troops were blocking them. Santa Claus could not get through either."

"Oh, yes he could, if he really wanted to," snapped Minnie. "He can fly onto rooftops and go over the whole world in one night. He is a mean old thing. I don't like him."

"Perhaps he had a good reason," said Aunt Sarah. "Maybe we shouldn't be angry at him until we find out. Tomorrow we will write to General Lee. Maybe he can tell us where Santa Claus has been. Now go to sleep and dream your dreams."

Aunt Sarah kissed Lutie, Birdie, and Minnie. She blew out the candles and shut the door. "I cannot remember what Santa Claus even looks like," said Minnie sadly.

"Sure you do," said Lutie. "Remember the poem I read you. It described him. Let's see if I can remember that part."

He was dressed all in fur from his head to his foot,
And his clothes were all tarnished with ashes and soot:
A bundle of toys he had flung on his back,
And he looked like a peddler just opening his pack.
His eyes how they twinkled! His dimples, how merry!
His cheeks were like roses, his nose like a cherry;
His droll little mouth was drawn up like a bow,
And the beard on his chin was as white as the snow.
The stump of his pipe he held tight in his teeth
And the smoke, it encircled his head like a wreath.
He had a broad face and a little round belly
That shook, when he laughed, like a bowl full of jelly
He was chubby and plump—a right jolly old elf:
And I laughed when I saw him, in spite of myself;

"Do you want to hear the rest, Minnie and Birdie?" asked Lutie.
The girls were already fast asleep. Lutie lay awake for a while,
thinking about General Lee. "Would such a famous man answer
their letter?" she wondered. "He was probably too busy to do
such a thing." Before long, Lutie was also off to dreamland.

Chapter 3

Lutie Shares Her Dream

The next morning was Saturday, but the girls still jumped out of bed early. They quickly changed from their nightgowns into their dresses. It was a chilly morning, so they also put on sweaters and warm stockings. They ran into their mother's room and gave her a big kiss. Then they hurried down the stairs to eat breakfast.

"I have a wonderful dream to tell," shouted Birdie.

"Me too," exclaimed Minnie.

"Wait until you hear mine," hollered Lutie.

Aunt Sarah greeted them with big bowls of warm grits smothered with butter, dried fruit, and milk. She had heard their excitement while they were coming down the stairs. "Finish your breakfast, and then we will go sit by the fire and listen to your dreams," she said.

They ate quickly and then joined Aunt Sarah by the warm fire. They all began speaking at once. Even children with good manners sometimes forget them when they are excited. Their aunt quieted them. "One at a time my dear children," she said. "Lutie will go first because she is the oldest."

"I was thinking about General Lee when I went to sleep last night," said Lutie. "Do you believe he actually showed up in my dream?

"I was walking through this big field," she said. "I could see the light of a fire up ahead. Someone rode toward me on a horse. He asked me if I was lost. He let me ride behind him on the horse to the campfire. Soldiers from our Confederacy were resting and singing songs. One young man in a gray uniform with holes in the jacket and pants said, 'Who do you have there, General Lee?' I could not believe what I was hearing. I was riding with the famous Southern general. The general helped me off the horse and sat down beside me in front of the warm fire."

"Did he know who you were?" asked Minnie.

"I told him my name, and he was so kind," said Lutie. "He offered me some bread. It wasn't very much food, but he said the soldiers were running out of supplies. I could see one man with holes in the bottom of his boots and another with his head wrapped in a bandage.

"I felt sad until I heard them talking," continued Lutie. "They talked about what an honor it was to be fighting for their homeland. And that it was their duty to fight wherever they were needed. They missed their wives and children, but they would go into battle whenever their general called them. It made me so proud of all of them. They were fighting for our South and for the things they believed in. I had so many questions to ask General Lee, but the next thing I felt was Birdie kicking me under the covers. My dream went away. It sure was exciting anyway."

"It would be great to meet General Lee," said Minnie. "When father came to visit, he always said good things about the general. I still wish he hadn't surrendered to the North, though."

Aunt Sarah ignored Minnie's comment. "That was a good dream, Lutie," she said. "Minnie, would you like to tell us your dream next?"

Chapter 4

Minnie and Santa

"My dream was sad and happy too," said Minnie. "I dreamed our house was just as it used to be, with all the pretty things in it and my rocking horse and toy house. And dear Papa was there, laughing his big hearty laugh that made us so happy. Papa and I went and played in the newly mown grass. We got tired, so we lay down and took a nap."

Minnie continued, "When I woke up, Papa was gone. I started to cry. Soon Santa Claus was standing there in his fluffy red suit. 'Where's my Papa?' I asked. Santa told me he had to go away. 'I don't want you here,' I cried. Santa explained that Papa was always watching over me."

" *'Why are you here?'* I asked.
" *'I heard that you don't like me,'* he answered.
" *'You are a mean old man who doesn't like the Rebel children,'* I shouted.

" 'I am sorry you feel that way,' he said. 'Let's go for a ride, and I will tell you all about it.' We walked around a clump of trees and found a big old sleigh and Santa's frisky reindeer. They were so cute. I just wanted to run and play with them. Next to the sleigh was a gigantic red-and-white balloon with a basket attached.

"Santa asked me which one I wanted to ride in. The sleigh and reindeer looked like fun, but I chose the balloon. Santa helped me get into the basket. Before I knew it, we were floating high above the rooftops, over the trees, and way across the river. It was the most wonderful feeling I ever had. The wind was blowing in my hair. No wonder Papa loved ballooning so much.

"Santa began to tell me where he had been for the past four years. I was trying to listen but also was watching everything on the ground. I spotted a horse running across a meadow. I leaned way over to watch it gallop. Suddenly, I tumbled out of the basket. I was screaming and doing somersaults in the air. Then, with a jolt,

I woke up from my dream. There I was. Safe in my big fluffy bed."

"But, Minnie, what did Santa say?" questioned Birdie. "Why hasn't he been here? Is he coming this year?"

"I don't know what he was saying," said Minnie. "I was more excited about my ride. I will wait up for him this year. If he comes, maybe he will take me for a ride in his sleigh this time."

"You don't sound as angry at Santa, Minnie," said Aunt Sarah. Minnie just smiled and didn't answer.

17

Chapter 5

Birdie and the Rainbow

Birdie was glad it was finally her turn to talk.
"I didn't meet General Lee or Santa Claus,
but you will like what I saw," she said.

"I dreamed that it had been a very hot day, and
then we had a rain shower. After the shower, Lutie,
Minnie, and I walked to the top of the hill on the
other side of the house. When we got there,
we saw a beautiful rainbow. The end of it seemed
to stop at the bottom of the hill. Minnie said we
should find out what was at the end of the rainbow.
So we ran down the hill, and guess what that
rainbow was made of?"

"What did you find, Birdie?" asked her aunt. "Was it different colored ribbons?"

"No, no," said Birdie, laughing and clapping her hands. "It was all kinds of candy. The white was cream, the pink peppermint, the yellow lemon, and the purple chocolate. When we found out it was candy, we all began nibbling at once, just as hard as we could. Then we heard a noise. A tiny little lady, dressed in all the colors of the rainbow, was sliding down the rainbow toward us.

"Lutie told us that it was Iris, goddess of the rainbow. We knew she would be mad and scold us. But before she could come close enough, I woke up. And that was my dream."

"What a yummy one it was,"
said Aunt Sarah.

Chapter 6

Writing to General Lee

After helping Aunt Sarah clean up the breakfast
dishes, the three girls wanted to go outside to play.
They went to find their coats, but before they could
put them on, it started to rain.

"Well, now what do we do?" asked Birdie
disappointedly.

"We were going to write to General Lee," said Lutie.
"Can we do that now?" she asked her aunt.

"Let me get my pen, ink, and paper," said Aunt
Sarah. "That sounds like a fine rainy-day activity."

The girls told Aunt Sarah all the things they wanted
to ask General Lee, especially about Santa Claus.
She then began to write the letter.

Dear General Lee,

We think you are the best man that ever lived. Our Aunt Sarah tells us you will go straight to heaven when you die because you are such a good person. We want to ask you a question. It's something that we want to know the truth about, and we know you always tell the truth.

Please, General Lee, tell us if Santa Claus loves the little Rebel children. We don't think he does. He did not come to the South for four Christmas Eves. Aunt Sarah thinks you did not let him cross the blockade lines. Is that true?

We all love you dearly. You are such a hero to all the people in the South. We want to send you something, but we don't have anything nice enough. We lost all our toys during the war. Birdie wants to send you one of our new kittens— the white one with black ears. Aunt Sarah thinks maybe you don't like kittens.

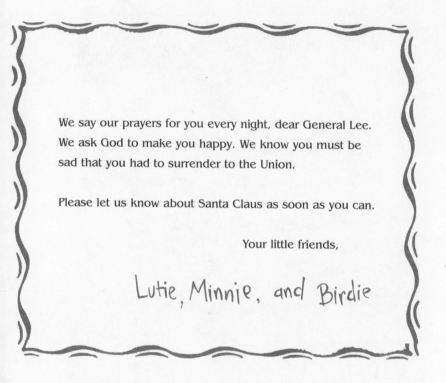

We say our prayers for you every night, dear General Lee.
We ask God to make you happy. We know you must be
sad that you had to surrender to the Union.

Please let us know about Santa Claus as soon as you can.

Your little friends,

Lutie, Minnie, and Birdie

The girls printed their own names on the bottom of the
letter. Aunt Sarah folded it, placed it in an envelope, and
sealed it with candle wax. The rain had stopped by then,
so they all bundled up and hurried out to mail their letter.

Chapter 7

A Speedy Reply

Every day after school, Lutie, Minnie, and Birdie
would run home quickly. They were eager to find
out if General Lee had answered their letter. They
knew he was a busy man, but surely he could take
time out for a simple reply. It would make them
so happy.

In about two weeks, they squealed with delight
when his letter arrived. Aunt Sarah settled them
down, then began to read:

My Dear Little Friends,

I was very glad to receive your kind letter. It is nice to know that I have the good wishes and prayers of three little girls named Lutie, Birdie, and Minnie.

I am very glad that you wrote about Santa Claus for I am able to tell you all about him. I can assure you that he is one of the best friends that the little Southern children have. You will understand this when I explain why he has not been to visit in the last four years.

The first Christmas Eve of the war, I was walking up and down the campground when I thought I heard a noise above my head. When I looked up, I saw the funniest looking old fellow riding along in a sleigh through the air. When I looked closer, I realized it was Santa.

"Stop! Stop!" I shouted. The funny fellow laughed but didn't seem as if he was going to obey me. I cried again, "Stop!" At that point he drove down to my side with a sleigh full of toys.

I told him he could go no farther South. He looked so disappointed.

"Oh what will my little Southern children do?" he said. I felt so sorry for him. I want little children to be happy too— especially at Christmastime. But I was certain of one thing. I knew my little friends would want me to do my duty rather than have all the toys in the world.

"Santa," I said, "take every one of the toys you have back as far as Baltimore. Sell them and use the money for things the soldiers need. Our soldiers have been fighting so hard to protect their homeland and their families. They never complain or ask for things. They consider it an honor to fight for the Confederacy. However, the sick and wounded need medicines, bandages, and ointments. The other soldiers could use good food, warm clothing, and even some new boots. The children will understand someday. I will explain it to them."

Santa Claus jumped into his sleigh and saluted me. "I always obey orders, General Lee," he shouted. And off he went to do his duty.

In a few hours he came sweeping down into camp again. Not only did he have everything I ordered, but also many other things our poor soldiers needed. And every Christmas, he took the toy money and did the same thing. The soldiers and I thanked him again and again. He gave clothing and food to many a poor soul who otherwise would have been cold and hungry.

Santa Claus is a good friend. I think of him as a hero of the war just like all the soldiers have been. I hope you will think about him that way, too.

I would be pleased to hear from you again, my dear little girls. I hope you will always consider yourself children of the South, but remember that, first, we are all Americans. We must all work together to rebuild this great country of ours.

I want you always to consider me your true friend.

R E Lee

P.S. I do like kittens, Birdie, but I already have two of my own, so I don't need another one.

"Hurrah! Hurrah!" shouted the girls when Aunt Sarah finished reading the letter. They all looked over her shoulder to see where the general had written his name.

"This is so exciting," said Lutie. "Let's go read the letter to Mama. Wait until my friends hear that General Lee wrote to us. I must tell them all about Santa Claus and the good things he did."

"Santa probably gave food and clothing to Papa one of those years," said Minnie. "I will never be angry at Santa again. He is a good person just like General Lee."

"Now that the war is over, do you think Santa will be here this Christmas, Aunt Sarah?" asked Birdie.

"We will have to wait and see," said Aunt Sarah. "In the meantime, we must be proud of General Lee and Santa Claus for all they did for the brave soldiers."

"God bless them both forever!" hollered Minnie. Lutie and Birdie shook their heads in agreement.

Chapter 8

A Guest at the Door

On the day before Christmas, the girls were singing holiday songs and decorating the mantel with branches they had just gathered. Aunt Sarah had helped Mama come downstairs. Wrapped in a warm blanket, she watched the girls from her big chair. The smells of cinnamon and chocolate drifted from the kitchen where Aunt Sarah was baking.

The girls stopped singing long enough to realize that someone was coming up the pathway. "Maybe it's Santa," hollered Minnie, as she ran to find out.

"He doesn't come to the door," Lutie reminded her.

Lutie and Birdie ran after Minnie to open the heavy door. There, to their amazement, stood a big man in wrinkled and torn clothing. He was grinning from ear to ear through his dark-brown beard and mustache. He looked like Papa. Lutie and Birdie weren't sure.

Minnie had no doubts. "Papa!" she hollered as she threw her arms around his neck. Then Lutie did the same thing. Little Birdie hesitated. She was so young when he left that it was hard to remember him.

Papa came inside. He hugged Mama and Aunt Sarah as tears flowed down their cheeks. Once everyone recovered from the shock, they sat by the fireplace to hear his story.

"I was floating in my balloon across Virginia," he said, "trying to see where the Union troops were camping, and the wind blew me off course. The Union soldiers shot down the balloon. I was spinning round and round in the basket. When I woke up, I was in a small farmhouse. A family had found me on the ground. I couldn't remember who I was or where I came from."

"Didn't you remember us?" asked Minnie.

"Not at that time," Papa said. "The family gave me food and a place to sleep until my old memories had returned and I could come home."

As they sat munching on cookies and drinking punch,
the family hugged and cried some more. There was so much
to talk about, so many questions to ask. Minnie gave Papa
a gigantic hug. "I surely believe that Santa loves us now,"
she exclaimed. "He brought us the best present ever."

~ The End ~

About Stratford Hall

A portion of the royalties from the sale of this book goes to Stratford Hall, the birthplace of General Robert E. Lee. The money will aid in preserving and maintaining the home that Lee remembered so fondly.

Stratford Hall, home to five generations of Lees, is situated on a high bluff overlooking the Potomac River. The large H-shaped house, dating from the late 1730s, sits surrounded by a complex of six original outbuildings on 1,670 acres in Virginia's historic Northern Neck.

In 1861, General Lee wrote to his wife:

"In the absence of a home I wish I could purchase Stratford. That is the only other place that I could go to, now accessible to us, that would inspire me with feelings of pleasure and local love."

Unfortunately, Stratford was not for sale,
so Lee was unable to realize his dream.

In 1929, the Robert E. Lee Memorial Association purchased the Stratford property and began restoring the building and gardens as a memorial to General Lee. Since that time, Stratford has been open to the public. A nonprofit organization committed to preservation, research, and education, the association depends on the generosity of a large number of supporters throughout the United States to fulfill its mission.

For more information about Stratford Hall Plantation,
please call (804) 493-8038

General Lee and Santa Claus
An Adaptation
by Randall Bedwell

An updated version of the original story
(written for today's children)
ISBN: 1-889709-01-8
Price: $9.95

General Lee and Santa Claus
by Louise Clack

An 1867 children's book,
reprinted in 1996
(written in 19th-century vernacular)
ISBN: 1-55793-106-2
Price: $9.95

May I Quote You, General...?

These are men of history and of legend, the South's great generals: Robert E. Lee, James Longstreet, Nathan Bedford Forrest, Stonewall Jackson. The way of life they defended is gone forever, but their names and words endure.

While each of them was a loyal son of the South, many of their statements reveal the individuals who were overwhelmed by the events of their time, and understandably so. The were literate, well-educated, thoughtful men, and the collection of statements in each of the books in this series shows the complexity for their thoughts and motivations — unfiltered by our modern preconceptions of what sort of people they were.

These four volumes are the first in the "May I Quote You, General?" series, which will contain the wisdom of generals on both sides of the conflict. Each 96-page book is available for $7.95 from Spiridon Press. Call 1-800-472-0438. Books may also be purchased via secured credit card transaction on the World Wide Web at www.spiridon.com

May I Quote You, General Lee?

May I Quote You, Stonewall Jackson?

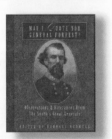

May I Quote You, General Forrest?

May I Quote You, General Longstreet?

 PUBLISHED BY CUMBERLAND HOUSE PUBLISHERS